BG

GOLD!

The Klondike Adventure

The life of a Klondike miner was often painfully lonely. In 1896, a prospector might search for gold for days without meeting another person.

GOLD!

The Klondike Adventure

Delia Ray

LODESTAR BOOKS
E. P. Dutton   New York

For my faithful, undercover editors
Bobby, Eddie, Carolyn, and Matt

Library of Congress Cataloging-in-Publication Data

Ray, Delia.
    Gold!: the Klondike adventure/Delia Ray; illustrated with
photographs.
        p.   cm.
    "Lodestar books."
    Includes index.
    Summary: Recounts the quest for and finding of gold in
the Klondike region of the Yukon Territory of northwestern
Canada (1896–1898), an event that brought joy to some,
heartbreak to many, and adventure to all.
    ISBN 0-525-67288-5
    1. Klondike River Valley (Yukon)—Gold discoveries—
Juvenile literature.   [1. Klondike River Valley (Yukon)—
Gold discoveries.]

I. Title	89-31823
F1095.K5R38 1989	CIP
971.9'1—dc20	AC

Published in the United States by E.P. Dutton,
a division of Penguin Books USA Inc.

Published simultaneously in Canada
by Fitzhenry & Whiteside Limited, Toronto

Produced by Laing Communications Inc.,
Bellevue, Washington. Design by Sandra J. Harner.

Printed in the U.S.A.   First Edition   10 9 8 7 6 5 4 3 2 1

Jacket photos
front: Photo by Mizony; Yukon Archives.
back: Photo by Kinsey & Kinsey; Ronald C. Kinsey, Jr.
        Collection.

Contents

Robert Henderson

I

Quest for Gold

R obert Henderson peered down at the sand settled in the bottom of his pan. Nothing. There was not a trace of gold. He stretched his tired back, pushed his broad-brimmed miner's hat up on his forehead, and stepped away from the stream that rippled by. It was time to pack up his supplies and try his luck on another creek.

For two years Henderson had wandered the Indian River Valley looking for gold. His search had led him into the heart of the Yukon Territory, a wild and rugged region in the far northwest corner of Canada. People were scarce in the Yukon. In 1896 a man could hike for days without ever seeing another human being. Only Indians, fur traders, and gold miners dared to live in a place so near the Arctic Circle, where temperatures dropped as low as 70 degrees below zero in the winter.

Robert Henderson looked as though he could withstand the coldest of winters. He was tall and wiry, hardened by months of toil and meager meals of beans and bacon. With his deep-set eyes, scowling brow, and stony face, he sometimes appeared cold and unfriendly. Yet Henderson was not a loner at heart. He often thought of seeing his family in the United States. Unfortunately, the journey home was long and dangerous. The nearest American city was 1,600 miles away. The miners even called civilization the Outside, as if the comforts of city life existed on another planet.

Henderson remembered the summer two years earlier when he had decided to leave the Outside. He had been working in the silver mines of Colorado, where he listened to his fellow workers spread tales about riches in the far North. Most men were content just dreaming about gathering gold nuggets like seashells on the beach. But Henderson was different. He said good-bye to his wife and children and set out for Canada to learn whether the rumors were true.

The difficult journey over steep mountain passes and through a maze of rivers and lakes did not frighten Henderson. He had been traveling to faraway places in search of gold for almost twenty-five years. Even as a boy, "Robbie" looked for

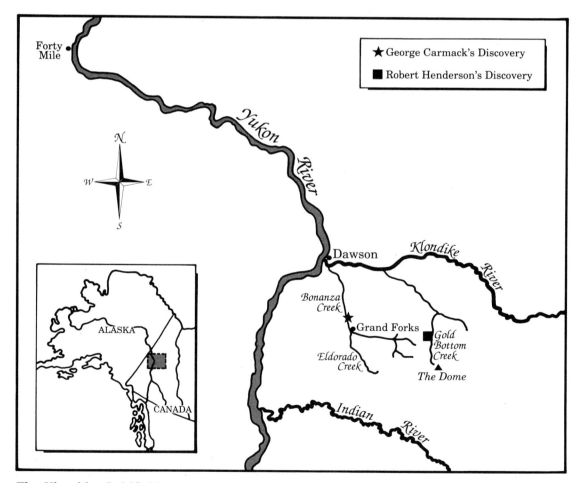

The Klondike Goldfields

nuggets in the rocky cliffs of Big Island, Nova Scotia—his childhood home that lay on the eastern edge of Canada overlooking the Atlantic Ocean.

There Henderson's father worked as a lighthouse keeper, guiding boats safely to port. Day after day Robbie watched ships sail into the harbor, fresh from their adventures at sea. Day after day he dreamed of setting out on his own voyages. At fourteen Robert Henderson vowed to spend the rest of his life looking for gold.

Working as a crewman aboard a sailing vessel, Henderson hunted for the gleam of yellow metal from New Zealand to Norway and other corners of the world. But even after years of traveling and tireless searching, he arrived in northern Canada with only ten cents in his pocket. Now, more than 3,000 miles away from where his quest began, Henderson was still haunted by hopes of finding gold.

As he stood beside the creek, Henderson gazed up at the highest hill in the distance. He had never crossed this ridge and explored the other side. Disappointed with the prospects nearby, Henderson climbed the Dome, as it was called, and looked down into the lush Klondike River Valley below.

From the top of the ridge, Henderson could see dozens of creeks and streams intricately connected like threads in a spider's web. Most of the creeks flowed into the larger Klondike River, which was known as the best salmon run in the territory. At the river the Indians caught their fish by hammering stakes into the sandy bottom and stretching nets between them. So, they called the river Thron-duick, a native word meaning "hammer-water." The miners, however, could not pronounce this strange word, and before long "Thron-duick" had changed to Klondike.

Henderson hiked until he came to a small creek where he paused to fill his pan with gravel. As he swished water back and forth in the pan, the lighter bits of sand and dirt washed away. His eyes widened. His stern features softened. There, shining against the dark iron, were bright yellow grains of gold—the most gold he had found since reaching the Yukon!

Convinced the ground beneath his feet was laced with riches, Henderson named the creek Gold Bottom. Soon he had recruited three other miners to help him shovel dirt into sluice-boxes. In a short time they collected $750 in gold. In 1896 this was a significant amount of money, considering how much it could buy Outside. A fine wool suit sold for only $10.00 and a pair of leather shoes for $1.75. A pound of bacon cost 40 cents and a pound of chocolate 75 cents. Even in the largest cities Outside, a good four-room apartment rented for just $1.25 a week.

In August Henderson realized that his flour, sugar, and

The miners shoveled gold-bearing dirt into long, wooden structures called sluiceboxes. Then they channeled stream water through the sluices to wash out dirt and gravel. The fine gold dust was left behind, settling in between the narrow poles or "riffles" on the floor of the boxes. In the photograph above, the man on the far right is holding a set of riffles.

other provisions were almost gone. He quickly set out for the nearest settlement to buy more. Once his moose-skin boat was packed tightly with supplies, Henderson returned to his camp by way of the Yukon River. As he reached the mouth of the Klondike, he spotted a small group on the bank, fishing for salmon and drying their catch on racks in the sun. It was George Washington Carmack and his Indian friends, Skookum Jim and Tagish Charley.

"There's a poor devil who hasn't struck it," thought Henderson as he poled his boat ashore. Naturally, he would spread word of his discovery. Henderson belonged to the Yukon Order of the Pioneers, a special club of lifelong miners who pledged to share news of a gold strike with anyone they met along the trail.

"What's the idea, Bob? Going hunting, fishing, or prospecting?" Carmack asked, as Henderson approached the campsite.

Carmack's round face remained expressionless as he listened to his visitor describe the discovery at Gold Bottom. Although Carmack was always interested in talk of the latest strike, he was not as obsessed as Henderson with finding gold. He was perfectly content to spend his days lazing beside the river or wandering from one salmon stream to the next.

The other miners shunned Carmack because he was not a devoted prospector and especially because he befriended the Tagish Indians. But Carmack ignored their unkind looks and prejudiced whispers. In fact, he was pleased when anyone remarked, "Why, George, you're getting more like a Tagish every day!" No statement could be more true. Carmack learned to speak tribal languages, married the daughter of the Tagish chief, and made the Indians his constant companions. He admired the bearlike strength of Skookum Jim, who supposedly once climbed eight miles of rocky mountainside with 150 pounds of bacon on his back. And he marveled at the quick reflexes of Tagish Charley, whom he described as "lean as a panther . . . and alert as a weasel."

Carmack sleepily considered the idea of hiking to Gold Bottom with Jim and Charley.

"What are the chances to locate up there? Everything staked?" Carmack asked, thinking other miners might already

The Yukon Order of the Pioneers, an organization of seasoned miners and respected businessmen, promised to treat fellow Klondikers kindly and always share the news of gold discoveries. The pioneers wore white sashes for special meeting days.

George Washington Carmack

have claimed the richest pieces of gold-bearing land.

Henderson glanced up at Jim and Charley, who were standing nearby.

"Well, there's a chance for you, George, but I don't want any Indians staking on that creek," he answered. With that abrupt remark, Henderson climbed back into his boat and disappeared up the Klondike River.

Of course, his thoughtless words angered the Indians. Skookum Jim complained loudly in his broken English. Charley looked at the ground. Carmack instead tried to brush the incident aside and turned his attention to the silver salmon flapping in his nets.

More than two weeks passed before Carmack finally decided to rouse his companions and look for Bob Henderson's claim. The threesome poled their boat two miles upriver and then set out on foot, plunging into the tangled underbrush surrounding Rabbit Creek. Traveling was difficult with their heavy packs full of mining tools. The hot August sun rose higher; thick clouds of mosquitoes swarmed around the men. Their moccasins sank in the marshy grasses, and thorny "devil club" plants pulled at their clothes. As Carmack later described, they emerged from the thickets feeling like "human pin cushions."

At each place they rested along the way, Jim and Charley casually dipped their gold pans into Rabbit Creek. To their surprise, heavy streaks of yellow appeared at the bottom of several pans. The Indians shouted with excitement and tried to persuade Carmack to stop and stake a claim. But he urged them on, convinced that the richest ground lay just over the next ridge.

Carmack and the Indians had just reached the top of the Dome when they spotted a curl of smoke rising from the purplish foothills below. Henderson's campfire! Skookum Jim still resented the prospector for his ugly remark. Carmack tried to soothe him, saying, "We've gotten this far. Let's go down and see what they've got." Since their dried fish and treasured supply of tobacco were running low, Jim did not need much encouragement.

Henderson and his partners were busy at work on their

Tagish Charley

Skookum Jim

claim when the three men trudged into the clearing. Carmack stooped to wash out several pans of gravel. Yet, none of the pans revealed prospects as rich as those the Indians had found on Rabbit Creek. The visitors' stomachs ached with hunger, but Henderson refused to part with any of his provisions—even after Jim and Charley offered to pay handsomely for food and tobacco.

This was strange behavior for a man who ordinarily made it his rule to help fellow miners through hard times. Clearly, Henderson's lack of hospitality was a sign of his dislike for the Indians. Ignoring Jim and Charley's angry faces, Henderson asked Carmack to send word if he found any valuable prospects on the way back to camp. Carmack agreed. But Henderson's unfriendliness was not easy for him to forget.

By the time they had walked a half mile past the fork of Rabbit Creek, the three men were too tired and hungry to hike any farther. Now their food was completely gone, so Jim set off through a spruce grove to hunt for game. In a short time he had killed a moose and was calling to Carmack and Charley to come see his prize. While waiting, Jim went to get a drink in the nearby creek. As he cupped his hand to scoop up the cool water, the Indian looked down in the sand. What he saw there would change his life forever.

Gold! More gold than he had ever seen in one spot. In Carmack's words, it was spread thick between the layers of rock "like cheese sandwiches." The partners threw down their backpacks and celebrated their discovery. Their happy cries echoed through the forest, and they performed a joyful dance of thanksgiving around the gold pan. As Carmack later recalled, it was a hilarious combination of a "Scotch hornpipe, Indian fox trot, syncopated Irish jig, and a sort of [Tagish] Hula-Hula."

In a few minutes Carmack panned out enough gravel to fill an empty Winchester shotgun shell with coarse gold. Then the three men sat down around the campfire for a feast of roasted moose meat. Later, while Jim and Charley slept, Carmack stared into the bed of glowing coals and imagined how he would spend his gold and his future. The more he thought, the more his love for the Indian way of life slipped away. He dreamed of a trip around the world, bank vaults full of money, a huge home with well-kept lawns and ornamental gardens. He dreamed of luxuries far, far away from the wilds of the Yukon where he had lived the last eleven years.

Early the next day Carmack marked off his claim. With a hand ax, he shaved the bark from a spruce tree and on the exposed surface, wrote:

To Whom It May Concern:
I do, this day, locate and claim, by right of discovery, five hundred feet, running up stream from this notice. Located this 17th day of August, 1896.

G. W. Carmack

Carmack then measured off claims for Jim and Charley. It

was time to head back to the settlement of Forty Mile to record his find and spread word of the great discovery. On the way, Carmack showed the gold-filled shotgun shell to each prospector he met and proudly gave directions to the creek he now called Bonanza.

Within two weeks, every valuable inch of Bonanza Creek was staked. The forest that once stood in peaceful silence was suddenly ringing with the sounds of excited voices shouting, huskies barking, axes pounding, and trees crashing to the ground. Men ran back and forth along the banks, wildly searching for unclaimed land. They huddled together to whisper stories of another discovery on a nearby creek called Eldorado, a stream that eventually produced millions of dollars in gold.

With each passing day, more newcomers arrived. Every miner in the region had heard the news, dropped his tools, and run to investigate the new strikes—every miner but one.

Robert Henderson was lifting another shovelful of dirt into the sluicebox when several men entered the clearing along Gold Bottom. He looked up, startled, and asked them where they had come from.

"Bonanza Creek," they replied.

Henderson paused for a moment. He thought he knew each hidden stream and waterway in the region, but he had never heard of Bonanza. When he asked for directions, the visitors pointed over the high Dome.

"Rabbit Creek!" Henderson exclaimed. "What have you got there?"

"We have the biggest thing in the world," one man said, his eyes lighting up.

"Who found it?"

"Carmack," they answered, puzzled that he hadn't already heard of the find.

Carmack! Henderson threw down his shovel and turned away. He sat down hard on the creek bank, so weak with shock

In the first months of the Klondike gold rush, miners were constantly spreading rumors of new discoveries on nearby creeks. One whisper could send dozens of fortune hunters racing off into the Klondike hills. These men, who are returning calmly from a stampede, probably had no luck in finding gold.

Most miners lived in crude, one-room cabins built from logs and covered with mud and moss. On the coldest days of winter, the miners rarely left the warmth of their cabins. Like many other Klondikers, these men even hung their laundry and panned for gold indoors.

and dismay that he could not speak. "How has this happened?" he asked himself bitterly. "Carmack would still be fishing for salmon on the Klondike River if I had not led him to the richest area in the Yukon."

Henderson did not remember how he had treated Jim and Charley, who were Carmack's closest friends. Instead, he remembered how he had obeyed the pioneers' code of honor and spread word of his own discovery, only to be betrayed.

There was no land left on Bonanza Creek for Henderson to stake. He began wandering again. The news of Carmack's discovery filled him with a gnawing restlessness. Although he found several creeks with promising prospects, each was poor compared to the wealth of Carmack's claim. Henderson was too tired and frustrated to continue. He finally purchased a ticket on a steamboat headed for the United States and the Outside.

Yet, Henderson had not seen the end of his bad fortune. As the harsh northern winter approached, the Yukon River froze, trapping the steamer between sheets of ice. Now Henderson's strenuous mining days began to take their toll. He became ill and required a doctor's care until the ice melted the following spring. With expensive medical bills to pay, the miner was forced to sell his only gold claim. Even the small sum he received for this sale was not safe. Thieves crept into Henderson's cabin on the ship and stole the very last of his Klondike gold.

When his ship finally reached the West Coast port city of Seattle, Washington, Henderson had one possession left to his name—the gold membership pin worn by the Yukon Order of the Pioneers. The miner walked the streets of the city, where he happened to meet an old friend. As they talked, Henderson suddenly tore the gold pin from his lapel and fastened it on his companion's vest.

"Here, you keep this," Henderson blurted out, his eyes filled with bitter disgust. "I will lose it, too. I am not fit to live among civilized men."

Eventually, Henderson returned to the life of a lonely miner. Although he could never overcome his deep disappointment, he also could not ignore his burning impulse to look for gold. After visiting his family for a short time, Henderson resumed his search. 🐾

The passengers of the Portland *arrived in Seattle with over two tons of gold and fantastic stories of the rich Klondike. Several of the miners in this photograph rest their sacks of gold on their shoulders.*

II

Klondike Fever

━━━━◦◦◦◦◦◦◦◦◦━━━━

T he city of Seattle was usually still asleep at daybreak on weekend mornings, but this Saturday large crowds of people rushed to the downtown waterfront at dawn. They shouted excitedly to one another, pointed across the water, and craned their necks to see. The *Portland* was coming! With its smokestack puffing and whistle blowing, the steamship chugged its way toward shore. On board was the most precious cargo ever to enter the Seattle harbor—sixty-eight miners from the Klondike and more than two tons of gold.

It was two days earlier when the first of the goldships had arrived in San Francisco, California. The steamer *Excelsior* had sailed into port, bringing its load of gold and the news that an even richer treasure ship was on its way to Seattle. Finally, the *Portland* appeared in Seattle on July 17, 1897—almost one year after George Washington Carmack and the Indians made their discovery on Bonanza Creek.

To the impatient spectators on the dock, the *Portland* seemed to move in slow motion. "Show us the gold!" yelled the onlookers, and several miners onboard lifted their heavy sacks for all to see. A thrill swept through the crowd, as each person imagined the glittering gold dust and nuggets inside the bags.

The big ship carefully pulled alongside the wharf and the gangplank was lowered.

When the first miner stepped into full view, the people stared in amazement. He heaved a buckskin bag to his shoulder and steadied the load. His face was lean and weather-beaten, lined with the strain of hard work and long Yukon winters. Behind him two men staggered down the ramp, each grasping the end of a sagging blanket. One after another they came, carrying old leather suitcases, pine boxes, and pickle jars— anything that would hold the heavy piles of gold. The commotion on the docks grew with each miner that appeared. "Hurray for the Klondike!" the people cried.

As the ragged and bearded men set foot on shore, they squinted into the crowd, searching for familiar faces. Instead of old friends and relatives, they were greeted by throngs of reporters eager for the story of the Golden North. Most of the miners tried to escape the newsmen with their persistent questions and headed for the best restaurant they could find. They ordered huge feasts with fresh fruit and vegetables, for many had been living on a diet of beans and flapjacks for months.

One of the reporters' favorite front page subjects was Clarence Berry, who had stepped off the *Portland* with $130,000 in gold nuggets. With his magnificent strength and honest ways, the broad-shouldered miner instantly became Seattle's hero. Berry had set out from California to find his fortune three years earlier, leaving behind his childhood sweetheart and a bankrupt fruit farm. When he reached Alaska, Berry joined forty other anxious goldseekers bound for the Yukon. The long winter journey over the mountains was harsh, and many in the group gave up in despair. More turned back when a fierce storm whipped up, destroying all of their supplies, but Berry pressed on. Of the forty goldseekers who began the trip, only he and two other men reached their final destination.

As the newspapers reported, Berry was not discouraged when he did not strike gold during his first year in the Klondike. He returned to California only long enough to marry his sweetheart, Ethyl Bush. Then back to the Yukon he went, with his new wife wrapped in a fur robe and bearskin hood.

Berry was working as a bartender in the saloon at the town of Forty Mile when George Carmack entered with his

18

Clarence Berry plays a fiddle with some friends in the Klondike, while a dog holds his hat.

shotgun shell full of gold dust. Berry threw down his apron and joined the stampede to the Klondike goldfields. Before long he had hired twenty-five workmen to help harvest the riches from his claim on Eldorado Creek. The gold lay thick, so thick that Mrs. Berry—as *The Seattle Times* reported—could walk through the diggings and pick up nuggets "as easily as a hen picks up grains of corn in a barnyard." In one season she gathered more than $10,000 in nuggets during her occasional strolls through the claim.

After the solitude of a rustic cabin in the North, the Berrys were not prepared for the swarms of reporters and followers that trailed them into restaurants and surrounded them on the street. The couple fled to San Francisco, but the crowds were just as curious there. The callers lined up outside the

Berrys' room at the Grand Hotel, until finally Mr. Berry allowed them to enter. Inside Room 111 was a glittering exhibition of gold. The visitors marveled over nuggets as big as chicken eggs and glass bottles full of gold dust, each labeled with the worth it contained.

In Seattle the excitement had reached a state of frenzy. The streets were packed with people who rushed downtown to celebrate the news from the North. Large groups gathered at banks and shop windows, where stacks of gold bricks and piles of shining nuggets were on display. One could not walk down the street without hearing the word *Klondike* spoken in a dozen different conversations.

The reason for this wild excitement was simple: The Klondike gold ships arrived during a time of terrible poverty for the United States. Thousands of businesses were closing, and millions of people had lost their jobs. It was not unusual to see a man die of hunger in the streets or a family pushed out of its home because of unpaid bills. This period of hardship, known as an economic depression, had lasted for several years and it seemed that it would never end.

The arrival of the *Portland* and the *Excelsior* was like a dream come true for the poverty-stricken nation. Penniless men read with delight each new tale of wealth in the daily papers. They read about William Stanley, who left Seattle as a poor bookshop owner and returned a millionaire. Now Stanley's wife could quit her job as a laundrywoman and order a whole new wardrobe of fancy clothes. They read about Tom Lippy, a former athletic instructor. He and his wife brought back $60,000 in gold—a fortune in 1897, when a full meal could be purchased for 25 cents. Everywhere, people were certain they could make a trip to the Yukon and strike it rich, just as William Stanley and Tom Lippy had.

The Klondike gold rush was on. "THE POPULATION IS PREPARING TO MOVE TO THE KLONDIKE" shouted the newspaper headlines. "EVERY MAN SEEMS TO HAVE CAUGHT THE KLONDIKE FEVER." Within hours after the gold ships had sailed into harbor, many men and women were quitting their jobs and preparing to head north. Seattle streetcar workers abandoned their trolleys on the track. Nuns left their churches,

and a quarter of the police force resigned. Even the mayor announced his resignation and promptly bought a steamboat for carrying passengers to the Klondike.

Firemen, store clerks, school teachers, lawyers, and doctors—workers from Seattle to San Francisco decided to trade their regular paychecks for picks and shovels. But the West Coast of the United States was not the only region to

A group of businessmen proudly display one and one-half tons of gold at the Alaska Commercial Company office in the Klondike. At today's prices, this amount would be worth well over ten million dollars.

In Seattle many merchants made fortunes selling equipment to goldseekers. Here, a group of future miners, ready to set out for the Klondike, stand in front of a wall of flour sacks and mining supplies.

be turned upside down by the Yukon discoveries. "Klondike fever" had spread to cities and towns throughout the country—and throughout the world. In New York, 2,000 people tried to buy tickets for the Klondike before the news of the gold strikes was one day old. Soon, groups of fortune hunters from Australia, Scotland, England, France, Italy, and other countries were also making their way toward the Yukon.

Many people could not afford to buy the steamship ticket

or the supplies needed to travel northward. However, there were other ways for a poor, but determined, man to join the gold rush. Often a more wealthy acquaintance, who could not make the trip himself, was willing to provide a "grubstake"—the money needed to buy provisions for the journey. In return, the Klondiker had to promise that he would pay his debt with a share of whatever gold he found.

The hardware stores and grocery counters were booming with business. In Seattle, San Francisco, and other West Coast port cities, goldseekers jammed store aisles. Never had

shopping lists been so carefully prepared. Each Klondiker wanted to face the Arctic winds and long journey ahead with the warmest clothes and most nourishing food that money could buy.

By the winter of 1897, Canadian government officials had passed a law forbidding anyone from entering the goldfields without enough supplies to last an entire year. Once a prospector had spent $500 to buy a year's worth of goods for the Klondike, his load weighed about 2,000 pounds. Many newspapers and guidebooks printed checklists of the exact items needed for a proper outfit, as the miners called their store of provisions. These were just some of the supplies that the future prospectors took along:

flour (150 pounds)	1 frying pan
bacon (150 pounds)	1 coffee pot
beans (100 pounds)	11 bars of soap
dried apples (25 pounds)	1 tin of matches
dried peaches (25 pounds)	1 box of candles
dried apricots (25 pounds)	1 medicine chest
rice (25 pounds)	1 pick
butter (25 pounds)	1 shovel
granulated sugar (100 pounds)	1 ax
coffee (15 pounds)	1 gold pan
tea (10 pounds)	1 handsaw
salt (10 pounds)	1 hatchet
pepper (1 pound)	6 towels
vinegar (1 gallon)	1 sheet-iron stove
1 tent	nails (16 pounds)

As the Klondikers waited for their hour of departure, they proudly sauntered up and down the streets in their new iron-toed boots and plaid flannel shirts. By now they were used to the scenes of confusion around them. The sidewalks were piled ten feet high with sacks of flour and crates of mining equipment ready to be sold to the next wave of stampeders. Long lines of people formed outside steamship offices, where the tickets were quickly sold out and clerks turned away hundreds of disappointed goldseekers. Dogs of every breed—

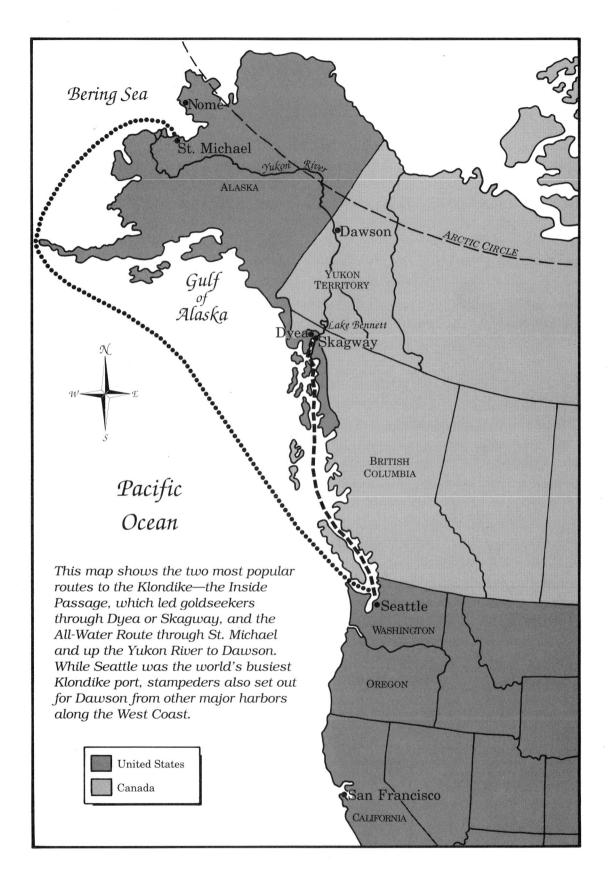

Bering Sea

Nome

St. Michael

Yukon River

ALASKA

Dawson

ARCTIC CIRCLE

YUKON
TERRITORY

Gulf
of
Alaska

Lake Bennett

Dyea Skagway

N
W E
S

BRITISH
COLUMBIA

Pacific
Ocean

*This map shows the two most popular
routes to the Klondike—the Inside
Passage, which led goldseekers
through Dyea or Skagway, and the
All-Water Route through St. Michael
and up the Yukon River to Dawson.
While Seattle was the world's busiest
Klondike port, stampeders also set out
for Dawson from other major harbors
along the West Coast.*

Seattle

WASHINGTON

OREGON

United States
Canada

San Francisco

CALIFORNIA

huskies, Labradors, Saint Bernards, and golden retrievers—ran barking through the streets with their owners chasing after them. Dogs had suddenly become very valuable possessions, for many would be trained to haul sleds full of supplies over the Klondike snow.

The stampeders often paused to watch street salesmen show off the newest products designed for those traveling north. There were Klondike medicine chests, Klondike blankets, and Klondike electric gold pans. There were portable Klondike houses, which the peddlers told their customers were "as light as air," even with the double bed and special Yukon stove that folded up inside. Dried food was sold in large quantities to future miners who wanted to save weight and space in their backpacks. Although most of the food was colorless and tasted bad, the miners bought everything from dried onions and turnips to evaporated rhubarb and potatoes.

Many dishonest merchants made money during the gold rush by selling worthless products or taking advantage of the innocent goldseekers. One Klondiker, Arthur Dietz, stopped on the street to watch a salesman pour some yellow powder from a sack and make a plate of scrambled eggs. Dietz was so impressed that he bought 100 pounds of the evaporated eggs for him and his traveling companions. It was not until the group was well on its way to the Klondike that Dietz opened the sacks. He realized that the yellow powder inside was really not eggs at all. The deceitful salesman had switched sacks and sold him 100 pounds of corn meal.

Like Arthur Dietz, thousands of goldseekers would face many unexpected difficulties on the Klondike trail. Most of the fortune hunters rushed to buy their tickets without truly knowing where their journey would lead them or what obstacles lay ahead. They read guidebooks about the Klondike, but even these were often inaccurate and misleading. Several books told readers that the Klondike was located in Alaska, when actually the region lay just across the Canadian border. Other travel guides incorrectly led readers to believe that the trails to the Klondike were like winding country lanes.

Many people also had unrealistic ideas of what their lives would be like once they reached the Klondike. One man set

Many businesses profited from the world's fascination with the Klondike. Eager fortune hunters paid the Yukon Mining School for lessons in driving dog teams, panning for gold, and using sluiceboxes.

out for the Yukon as if he were taking a pleasant northern vacation. His outfit included thirty-two pairs of moccasins, one case of pipes, two Irish setters, a puppy, and a badminton set. Another man, who worked as a dance instructor, had hopes that he could give dancing lessons to the miners and Indians of the North, while digging nuggets during his spare time in the summer. A woman from Ireland planned to move

27

As steam from the ship's boilers fills the air, passengers look down on
hundreds of friends, relatives, and spectators who jam the docks,
waiting to see the Humboldt leave for the Klondike.

her entire family to the Yukon, where she imagined her sons and daughters would attend school in the daytime and dig gold in the early mornings and late evenings. None of these Klondikers expected the harsh Arctic climate or understood that, to make any money, gold digging had to be a full-time job.

No one had more impractical ideas of how to become wealthy in the Klondike than the businessmen, scientists, and inventors of the day. The newspapers were full of advertisements for strange new inventions that were "guaranteed" to make gold mining easier and pockets fuller. A business called the Trans-Alaskan Gopher Company promised to train gophers to claw through the icy gravel and uncover nuggets of gold.

Another scheme was the "Klondike Bicycle." Its inventor, Jacob Coxey, told reporters that his special bike could carry 500 pounds of supplies all the way to the Yukon. With its unfolding sidewheels, handlebar attachments, and rawhide-bound frame, the unsuccessful Klondike Bicycle was a comical looking vehicle. Certainly, if Jacob Coxey had ever seen the Yukon's steep mountains and dense forests, he never would have invented such an odd contraption.

As the summer of 1897 passed, a new ship left for the Klondike almost every day. The goldseekers boarded the most unusual assortment of boats ever assembled. Coal ships, yachts, schooners, barges, and old fishing boats—any vessel that could float became a goldship. Many boats that had long ago been declared unsafe were quickly brought in from the shipyards. Even with the hasty repairs that were made, many Klondike boats were referred to as "floating coffins."

Despite warnings, the excited stampeders did not seem to care whether their boats were seaworthy or not. The gold-crazed people pushed up the ramps, filling every available space onboard. Passengers stood elbow-to-elbow. Over the ships' railings, several tearful faces appeared. Many goldseekers would not see their families again for months and months. But as the crowd below cried, "Three cheers for the Klondike!" and the ship whistles blasted a farewell, most of the passengers forgot their sadness.

Their Klondike adventure had finally begun. ❧

Day after day, stampeders climbed the steep Chilkoot Pass with slow steps, bending painfully under the weight of their heavy loads.

III

The Journey North

━━━━◦◦◦◦◦◯◦◦◦◦◦━━━━

By the time the gold rush began, prospectors had been searching for the best way to reach the Klondike for almost thirty years. They struggled over jagged peaks, crossed wide canyons, and forged new trails through dark swamps and forests. No mountain was too high to climb if the Golden North waited on the other side.

When news of the discoveries spread in 1897, the search for the easiest and fastest route to the Klondike became more frantic. Guidebooks and transportation companies bombarded the stampeders with travel recommendations, each suggesting a different path to the goldfields. Thousands of fortune hunters struck out on unknown trails that only led to danger and hardship.

One group of goldseekers set out for the Klondike by way of the great Malaspina Glacier, near the southern border of the Yukon Territory. Nineteen men found themselves on the frozen shores of Alaska, facing a shimmering ice field that seemed to stretch forever. For three months the weary travelers fought to cross the treacherous glacier with its slippery surface and hidden crevasses. Three members of the party and four sled dogs fell to their deaths in the deep cracks that yawned open in the ice like huge jaws.

More dangers lurked on the other side of the glacier. The travelers lost their way in a dense mountain forest, where thick

brambles blocked the path and shut out all sunlight. When the food supply ran low, the men choked down raw beans to survive. They had forgotten all thoughts of finding gold. Their only desire was to find warmth and safety. But that meant tracing their steps back across the Malaspina ice field.

One year after they began their journey, the men staggered to the shores of the Pacific Ocean, where they were rescued by a passing ship. Only four men had survived the terrifying expedition. Two had been permanently blinded by the burning glare of the sun on the ice.

Not all northern routes were as perilous as the Malaspina trail. Stampeders could choose from two other popular routes, which quickly became known as the safest ways to reach the Klondike. In the fall of 1897, almost 2,000 fortune hunters bought tickets for the all-water route. These Klondikers boarded

Some unreliable guidebooks even instructed stampeders to cross treacherous glaciers like the one shown here. In this photograph, a woman uses a pole to pull a man from a crevasse.

ships in West Coast port cities and sailed to the mouth of the Yukon River in western Alaska. There, the passengers were met by riverboats and ferried upstream to the city of Dawson near the goldfields.

Although it was nicknamed the "rich man's route," this expensive voyage was nothing like a luxury cruise. From Seattle, the Klondike was almost 5,000 miles away by water—a distance that often seemed endless to the impatient passengers. Many boats reached the Yukon in the midst of winter after the river had frozen into a solid sheet of ice. Hundreds of stampeders were stranded along the beaches until the ice melted the following spring.

Most goldseekers could not afford the $1,000 ticket for the all-water passage. They followed a much more exhausting route to the Klondike. This journey also began with a steamship ride north, but the sea trip ended abruptly at Alaska's southern coast. Passengers were hurriedly unloaded at the waterfront towns of Skagway or nearby Dyea. Once ashore, the stampeders collected their belongings and slowly pushed their way inland, struggling over the mountains to the Yukon Territory. To reach the goldfields, the Klondikers then built boats and sailed more than 500 miles down the Yukon River.

It was this route that became the busiest highway to the Klondike. The sealanes off the Pacific coast grew crowded with the traffic of Alaska-bound ships. Captains ordered their vessels full speed ahead, stubbornly trying to pass other steamers and take the lead. However, most of the ramshackle boats heading northward were so overloaded that they moved through the waves like water-logged tubs.

Every available space aboard the Klondike ships was filled. The decks were crammed with crates of food, wooden sleds, tents, pack animals, and bales of hay. Deep in the hull of the *Islander*, 600 horses were wedged tightly together in long rows—so tightly that they could not lie down or move away from the ship's hot engines. As the shrill whistles blasted and the engines began to pound, the horses reared back on their harnesses, biting and kicking in terror.

The passengers on the *Islander* were not much better off than the horses. During one of its voyages to Alaska, the

As the steamship Willamette *prepares to leave port, men climb the riggings of the grimy coalship and stand on bales of hay for a better view. With more than 800 passengers and 300 packhorses aboard, there was barely enough room to move about on the decks.*

Islander sailed into a fierce storm with high winds. The ship began to pitch violently, and the captain changed his course, heading for the refuge of a small inlet called Safety Cove. Just as the anchor was dropped, the vessel's water supply ran completely dry. The passengers were thrown into a state of panic. In the words of one witness, "the women wept, men cursed and prayed" as their lips grew more parched. Soda water, beer, and wine were guzzled down. Finally, in utter desperation, the men drank catsup and Worcestershire sauce from the bottle. Even the dogs on board were crazy with thirst.

They began to yelp and howl uncontrollably. The passengers' terror grew when these howls were answered by the cries of wild animals on the shores of Safety Cove.

Goldseekers on other vessels had their own hardships to bear. In August, more than 800 stampeders crushed their way aboard the *Willamette*, an old coal carrier bound for Dyea. Only a few hours before the ship's departure, workmen had hastily shoveled tons of coal from the lower decks. In its place carpenters built rough wooden bunks for the first-class travelers. Yet, no one had taken the time to sweep out the coal dust left behind. Now every passenger and every surface was coated with the dirty, black dust.

The situation only grew worse once the *Willamette* was underway. Chaos broke out in the ship's dining room. The eating area was small and cramped, with space for only sixty-five diners. Hungry passengers formed long lines for meals, but many quickly lost their appetite when they saw the revolting food being served. To make matters worse, the smell of the 300 packhorses and their dirty stalls followed the stampeders wherever they went. Some tried to escape the sickening smell by sleeping. Second-class passengers without bunks even slept in lifeboats strapped to the ship's upper decks.

Despite these hardships, many passengers tried to make the best of the uncomfortable steamship journey. They held boxing matches, poker tournaments, and sing-alongs with fiddle music. One goldseeker, Mont Hawthorne, fondly remembered how the passengers on his ship gathered on deck for daily exercise. "We'd line up behind each other, and each fellow would put his hands on the shoulders of the one ahead of him," Hawthorne described. "Then we'd run 'round and 'round the deck, yelling to each other and laughing. . . .We didn't dare get soft, for we was hitting the trails as soon as we got off the boat."

As their steamers sailed closer to Alaska, the stampeders talked of nothing but "hitting the trails." They lounged about on bales of hay in their new buckskin suits and mining gear, discussing the upcoming journey. They inspected one another's camping supplies as if examining the finest silks from China. Passengers who had been strangers when the sea voyage began

now decided to become partners and face the dangers ahead together.

All through the summer of 1897 and the following year, one steamship after another puffed into Skagway Bay in southern Alaska. The vessels, which were too large for the shallow waters near land, anchored in the open canal. A fleet of rowboats, Indian canoes, and barges rushed out to meet the steamers and carry the passengers and their freight ashore.

As the crew unloaded the cargo, the goldseekers watched

On the beaches of Skagway and Dyea, goldseekers had to search through mountains of mining supplies to find their own outfits.

in dismay. Their precious mining supplies were heaved over the side of the ship carelessly, landing with a crash on the barges below. Horses, sheep, and oxen were dumped, terrified and kicking, into the icy water and forced to swim ashore.

Before long, a mountain of supplies began to rise up on the beaches. The Klondikers wandered frantically through the jungle of brassbound trunks, flour sacks, Yukon stoves, and shipping boxes. Desperately, they tried to find their own outfits before the goods were soaked by the incoming tide.

When the stampeders had gathered their belongings, they noticed the strange scene around them. Beyond the beach

In Skagway, men hurried up and down the muddy main street, making last-minute preparations for the difficult trek over White Pass.

stretched acres of white tents and rickety shacks. This was Skagway—a muddy town of makeshift buildings and restless men. The goldseekers flowed down the main street in an endless stream, past the tent saloons, blacksmith's shed, and doctor's shanty. None of the stampeders paused for long. Every moment wasted meant one less panful of gold.

There were few routes to the Klondike that tried men's patience more than the Skagway Trail over White Pass. The trail began harmlessly with a smooth wagon road through campsites and cottonwood groves. But just as the goldseekers began to settle into an easy pace, the pleasant pathway turned into an obstacle course of shaky rocks, horseshoe turns, and knee-deep bogs.

Forty-five miles of back-to-back hills stood between the stampeders and the Yukon River. The first hurdle was Devil's Hill, a frightening climb over moss-covered boulders and down steep ravines. Then came Porcupine Ridge, with its cliffs and ledges. At the top of Summit Hill lay the border between Alaska

and Canada. Yet, many travelers did not even attempt to cross it. When they saw the peaks still left to climb, they turned back in weary defeat.

It was impossible to carry a year's worth of supplies over White Pass in a single trip. So, the Klondikers hauled their outfits across the mountains piece by piece. An average man could carry only about fifty pounds at once. If he did not have a pack animal, it sometimes took forty trips to move his entire outfit over the mountain. As thousands tramped back and forth with their heavy bundles and backpacks, they churned the trail into a river of oozing mud. Wagon wheels and heavy boots sunk into the mire like hot knives in butter. The path was

Travelers on the Skagway Trail had to cross huge boulders and sharp rocks. Although those with packhorses often searched for ways to avoid these obstacles, no path was completely safe.

so narrow that if one person got stuck in a mudhole no one could pass, and the trail backed up for miles.

The Klondikers used a wide assortment of devices to haul their outfits over White Pass. They trudged along, pushing wheelbarrows, handcarts, and other awkward inventions. One woman drove a sleigh pulled by six Angora goats. Another man scrambled to balance a giant wheel he had built with loading platforms on either side. Whenever this contraption hit a bump, the entire load came tumbling down.

Jack London, an ex-sailor who went on to write the famous novel *The Call of the Wild* and many other adventure books about the North, also joined the rush over White Pass. In a letter describing the frustration of carrying 1,000 pounds of supplies along the rough trail, London wrote, "For every mile . . . I will have to travel from 20 to 30 miles." Like many

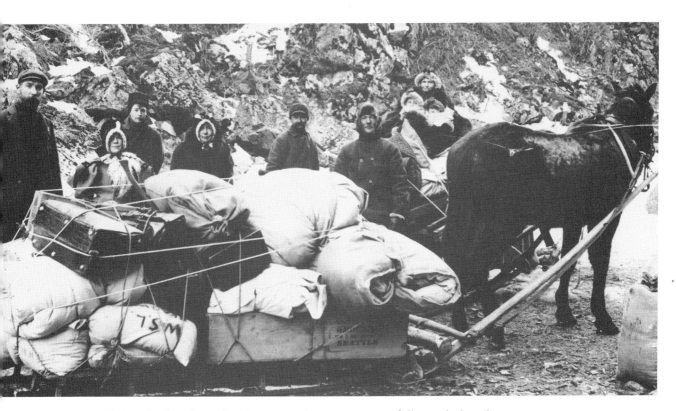

Not only hardened miners and strong men followed the dangerous Skagway Trail. As this photograph shows, entire families—even grandmothers and small children—joined the rush over White Pass.

The bodies of fallen packhorses filled the ravines along the Skagway Trail.

other goldseekers, London was forced to return home empty-handed when he became snowbound and fell ill from a lack of nourishing food.

If the Skagway Trail was difficult for the goldseekers, it was a nightmare for horses. By the end of 1897, 3,000 packhorses had been forced to join this strange parade over White Pass. Most of the animals were old, decrepit, and painfully thin. Some horses, as a witness described, "looked as if a good feed of oats would either break their backs or make them sag beyond remedy." Yet, the gold-crazy stampeders did not hesitate to heap pack saddles and knapsacks on their horses' bony spines. One thoughtless owner was seen piling more and more supplies on his donkey's back, until the poor creature finally crumpled to its knees.

With their flanks trembling and eyes wide with fright, the horses struggled to find a foothold in the razor-sharp rocks. They stumbled on the slick granite, scraping their legs raw.

They floundered through swamps and sank to their tails in the black muck.

As the trail climbed higher, the dangers grew. Every day several horses strayed too close to the edge of the cliffs and plunged to their deaths in the deep gorges below. Some people claimed that these falls were not always accidental. Tappan Adney, a newspaper reporter, met a man who had watched a horse leap off the edge of Porcupine Hill. The man insisted the horse had committed suicide rather than face the tortures ahead.

White Pass soon became known as the "Dead Horse Trail." The path was littered with bones; the smell of rotting horse flesh filled the air. Still, the Klondikers pushed forward, stepping over the dead animals without a second look.

As the mad rush over White Pass continued, another trek across the mountains was taking place only three miles away. Each week a new group of stampeders arrived in the rough settlement of Dyea. Stepping ashore, they anxiously raised their eyes upward. Somewhere, high above the town, lay a narrow and windy gap in the mountains called the Chilkoot Pass—a gateway to the Yukon River.

On their way toward the Chilkoot Pass, these five determined women lift their skirts or ride piggy-back as they cross the shallow Dyea River.

Although the Dyea Trail was shorter than the Skagway route by several miles, the path climbed 600 feet higher and led steadily upward. As the path steepened, telltale signs of the hikers' exhaustion began to appear. A chest of china and silverware, a box of books, or a crate of canned peaches—items once considered treasures—now became useless burdens and were thrown down alongside the trail.

At the end of each day, the Klondikers plodded into weather-beaten camps scattered along the Dyea Trail. At Finnegan's Point, Canyon City, and Camp Pleasant, the travelers could strip their packs from their aching shoulders and find a level spot to rest for the night. If a man was too weary to gather firewood, pitch a tent, or cook his own meal, he headed for one of the wayside roadhouses. Most of these so-called hotels and restaurants were no more than large tents or wooden

Several roadhouses were scattered along the Dyea Trail, where travelers could stop for a meal or rest for the night. This roadhouse sold liquor, tobacco, and freshly made doughnuts and coffee.

shacks displaying handpainted cloth signs. Still, the stampeders flocked to the dirty way stations as if they were luxury resorts offering five-course dinners and feather beds.

At Sheep Camp the Palmer House fed and boarded almost 600 stampeders a day. Seventy-five cents paid for a turn to sit at a long plank table and gulp down a meal of beans, bacon, and tea. When supper was over, the tables were pushed back and the one-room restaurant became a hotel. The goldseekers took off their heavy boots, hung their filthy socks over the rafters, stretched out on the floor, and sank into a dreamless sleep. By nine o'clock at night, no one could walk across the tightly packed room without stepping on the sleeping men.

On clear mornings the guests at Palmer House awoke to their first glimpse of the Chilkoot Pass. The sight was so ominous that some stampeders immediately turned back. Rising up from the valley was a towering mountain wall. The passageway through the peaks lay at the top, above four winding miles of steep gray rock. To those who stood at the bottom of the gorge, the climb looked impossible. But there, in the distance, an endless line of stampeders marched their way to the summit like an army of black ants.

Winter never seemed to leave the Chilkoot Pass. From October to May, the slopes were blanketed in snow and ice. Huge glaciers hung from the jagged mountaintops, threatening to break off and hurl down into the gorge at any time. Beyond Sheep Camp, the trail was as slippery as glass. Packhorses became helpless on the frozen slopes, and many were abandoned at the foot of the mountain. Even sled dogs had to be carried across the pass in their owners' arms.

Long after the Klondike gold rush had ended, men and women still remembered every detail of crossing the Chilkoot Pass. They remembered the agonizing weight of their packs. They remembered hearing groans of fatigue and seeing others nearly collapse under the strain. One woman recalled the pathetic sight of "weak, old, even feeble ones, ascending the steep mountain with forms almost bent double."

A smooth rut was worn in the snow by thousands of shuffling feet. The goldseekers trudged up the mountain in single file. Most did not dare to step out of place. If a stampeder

From a distance, the line of stampeders climbing the Chilkoot looked like a black chain hanging down the mountain. When the climbers reached the top of the pass with one load of supplies, many slid back down to pick up another.

moved off the trail to rest, it sometimes took hours to break back into line. Near the summit, the trail became so steep that the Klondikers were almost crawling on their hands and knees. Finally, several ambitious men decided to improve the situation. With their axes, they hacked out 1,500 steps from the snow. Then they charged a toll to all who wanted to use these steps, which soon became known as the Golden Stairs.

In April of 1898, disaster struck the Chilkoot Pass. An avalanche came barreling down the mountain, burying nearly 100 stampeders under piles of wet, heavy snow. When the news spread to Sheep Camp, a crowd of rescuers grabbed shovels and rushed up the trail to the scene of the accident. Adolphe Mueller was trapped under the snow for three hours before he was finally uncovered. He described his ordeal: "I could not

Rescuers stare down at three unfortunate victims of the avalanche on Chilkoot Pass.

move a hand or foot. I was held as fast as if I were in a plaster . . . cast. I could hear people near me groaning and praying; but in only a few minutes all was still." More than sixty people died in their icy tombs. Many bodies were found frozen in the same positions that they had been trapped—running frantically from the thundering avalanche of snow.

Despite its dangers, the Chilkoot Pass could not conquer the spirit of the Klondikers. Some only grew more defiant as the difficulties of the Dyea Trail increased. Up the Golden Stairs they climbed, carrying every type of load imaginable. Canoes, crates of turkeys, and even a piano were packed on men's backs over the Chilkoot Pass. Captain A. J. Goddard and his wife carried a steamboat across the mountains piece by piece. One man who joined the gold rush weighed nearly 600 pounds. It soon became evident that he was too heavy to make the climb on foot, so he paid to be hauled over the pass strapped to a sled.

All through the winter the stampeders poured over the mountains, leaving the tortures of the Chilkoot and the White passes behind. But one last challenge faced the fortune hunters: the mighty Yukon River. The Dyea and Skagway trails ended at adjoining mountain lakes whose emerald-green waters fed into the Yukon. No boats waited along the shores of Lake Lindeman or nearby Lake Bennett to carry passengers to the Klondike. It was up to each man to build his own vessel and find his way 500 miles downriver to Dawson, the "City of Gold."

By the spring of 1898, 30,000 people were camped along the frozen lakes at the foot of the passes. In just a few months the stampeders had transformed this once-quiet valley into a bustling boat-building center. Acres of stumps stood where forests had once grown strong and green. The mountain hollows echoed with the sounds of falling timber and rasping saws. Among the piles of lumber and rows of half-built boats, the stampeders worked diligently. When the ice finally broke on the lakes, each man wanted to be ready to set sail.

One of the first steps of boat building was a long and tiring process called whipsawing. To make narrow boards for the sides of the boats, the stampeders placed fresh-cut logs

On the shores of Lake Bennett, men work at a whipsawing platform.

on a raised platform known as a sawpit. Whipsawing was a two-man job; while one man stood upon the platform, his partner took a place underneath. Each worker then grabbed the handle of a long, jagged-tooth saw and began guiding the sharp teeth up and down through the log.

Whipsawing ended countless friendships during the gold rush. The work was maddening. At each stroke of the saw, the man below received a face full of powdery sawdust. The man above felt his back wrench and his hands blister. They shouted and cursed, each convinced that the other was not doing his share of the work. Along the shores of Lake Bennett and Lake Lindeman, tempers exploded. Friends who had braved the entire journey together divided their outfits and went separate ways. In their foolish rage, some men split their boats

In the spring of 1898, the shores of the mountain lakes were crowded with thousands of newly built boats. Stampeders hurriedly put the finishing touches on their vessels, anxious to be off for Dawson.

in half. One story even told of partners who cut a frying pan in two.

On May 29, 1898, most of these squabbles were forgotten. The ice broke with loud cracks and the race to the goldfields resumed. In the next two days more than 7,000 boats pushed off the shore. There were crafts of every description: rafts, canoes, sailboats, tiny dinghies, and wide barges. One group had built its vessel like a Mississippi riverboat, using hand-cranked paddle wheels instead of oars to navigate.

As the spring wind swept the boats northward, each stampeder felt a thrill of excitement. This quickly turned to fear when the inexperienced boaters realized that the danger was not over. Miles of white-water rapids and hidden rocks

While these three goldseekers proudly called their sailboat Yukon Flyer, *most boat-builders named their vessels after their wives or girlfriends.*

lay ahead. The clumsy boats plunged into the rough waves, while the men fought wildly to steer away from boulders. A Seattle man was sucked into a whirlpool and his boat spun in a circle for several hours before he finally managed to break free. Many boats smashed to splinters on the rocks, dumping passengers and outfits overboard. From Lake Lindeman to

Many boaters lost control of their tiny vessels in the roaring waters that swept through Miles Canyon—one of the most frightening points of the Yukon River trip.

Dawson, the shores were lined with stampeders trying to mend their boats and dry their wet supplies in the sun.

Still the boat race continued. Every day a new group of stampeders set sail. As one man later wrote, "It was a sight long to be remembered. Hundreds of white sails moved like ducks across the lake. . . . We all wondered if there could possibly be enough gold in the Klondike for such an armada of stampeders." ❧

In the early days of the gold rush, many newcomers arrived in Dawson expecting to find a wealthy town with tidy shops and clean streets. Instead, they found confusion and rivers of mud.

IV

The City of Gold

———◄∙∙∙∙◦◦◉◦◦∙∙∙∙►———

T he first crate of eggs to arrive in Dawson caused more excitement than a bushel of gold nuggets. All through the bleak winter of 1897, the miners had lived on the brink of starvation. For months they had eaten nothing more than unsatisfying rations of beans.

Spring finally arrived, and the first boat of the season appeared amid the icebergs on the Yukon River. When the newcomer hit shore with a boatload of eggs, a shout rang out and the townspeople of Dawson came running. In less than an hour, the happy businessman had sold his entire stock of 2,000 "fresh" eggs at eighteen dollars a dozen.

Other enterprising traders were not far behind. They knew the miners were hungry and had gold to spend. They poled their boats through the cakes of ice like madmen, racing to bring the people of Dawson precious goods at high prices. They brought lemons and oranges, canned oysters, and ham. They brought kittens, bottles of ink, brooms, and rubber boots. Most amazing of all, they brought word that thousands of goldseekers were heading upriver for Dawson.

Each day several more boats dribbled in. A strange mood of anticipation filled the air. Some stampeders arrived with newspapers to sell. It made no difference that most of the papers were weeks old. After the long, lonely winter, the miners craved news from the Outside. One man was able to sell his paper for

fifteen dollars, even though it was soaked with bacon grease. That evening at the town hall, the paper was read aloud to hundreds of people who paid a dollar apiece to hear the news.

Suddenly, at the beginning of June, the trickle of boats turned into a flood. Canoes, rafts, and skiffs poured around the bend in the Yukon River at all hours of the day and night. Soon there were so many vessels lined up on the banks that men had to jump from boat to boat to reach the shore.

At four o'clock in the morning on June 8, the cry of "Steamboat!" echoed through the streets of Dawson. Someone had glanced downriver and spotted a tiny speck and a faint puff of smoke. As the vessel drew closer, its whistle began to blow

In the spring of 1898, the townspeople of Dawson gathered to hear a man read news of the Outside from the only American newspaper in town.

shrilly. All the dogs in Dawson joined in, lifting their voices in long, sorrowful howls. The first steamer of the year, loaded with passengers on the all-water route, had arrived.

When they saw the filthy streets of Dawson, some newcomers did not even get off their boats. One man pronounced the city "a regular mudhole of a place." He promptly put his outfit up for sale and headed for the Outside. Other newcomers were so eager to explore the new territory that they ran into town without tying their boats to shore. The old-timers of the community gathered at the waterfront to watch the inexperienced men. They called them cheechakos—an Indian word for newcomers. After spending most of their lives mining for gold, the old-timers observed these "tenderfeet" with a mixture of amusement and scorn.

Once the cheechakos had taken a quick look at Dawson, most grabbed their shovels and spread out over the countryside to find gold. They ran along the banks of the creeks, ready to stake their claim. Slowly, the terrible truth became clear. Every gold-bearing creek and hillside for miles around had been staked for months.

The newcomers were shocked with disappointment. Nothing in Dawson lived up to their expectations. The city was shabby. Finding work with good wages was difficult. And, a disease known as typhoid fever was killing dozens of people. In a letter to his wife, a Klondiker named R.W. Roberts wrote, "Should anybody ask you what I think of their coming here, tell them that my candid advice is for them to *stay where they are.*"

The newcomers' frustration grew as they paused to watch the happy miners at work. Many stampeders had arrived at the creeks during "spring clean-up"—a festive time in the mining season. After months of toil, the prospectors were finally collecting their rewards.

All winter long the miners had struggled to hit bedrock, the richest layer of ground that lay deep below the surface of the earth. It was impossible to cut through the frozen soil with shovels, so the miners built fires over their claims to thaw the hard ground. Inch by inch they scraped away layers of dirt and burrowed deeper into the shaft. The dirt was hauled to the surface in buckets and dumped into huge stockpiles. When the

To find the richest layer of ground, miners had to dig their way down to bedrock. But even after spending months at this difficult task, there was no guarantee that they would strike gold.

snow melted on the mountainsides and the creeks began to swell, the miners built dams to guide the icy runoff into sluiceboxes. Once they shoveled the dirt from the stockpiles into the boxes, spring clean-up began.

Clean-up had become a favorite social event in Dawson. Women attended the affair in full skirts, fancy hats, and sleek furs. For an outsider, it was strange to see groups of well-dressed guests picking their way across the rocky hillsides toward the claims. As the workers dumped the dirt into the sluiceboxes, the visitors lined up and down the long, wooden structures to watch the water come rushing through. Soon the glitter of fine gold appeared at the bottom of the boxes, much to the delight of the spectators.

Gold was not the only attraction at the clean-up. The guests were thrilled to rub shoulders with the rich claim-owners, who were known throughout the North for their fabu-

lous wealth. Antone Stander, Charley Anderson, Dick Lowe, Clarence Berry—two years earlier these men were merely faces in the crowd. Now they were Dawson's leading citizens, presiding over spring clean-up like kings holding court.

Perhaps the most famous of the mining giants was "Big Alex" McDonald. McDonald had arrived in Dawson too late to find an empty space on the richest creeks. When another miner became disgusted with his prospects and put his land up for sale, McDonald bought half of it for a sack of flour and some bacon. In one summer this small piece of land on Eldorado Creek produced $40,000 worth of gold. With this success, buying claims turned into an obsession for McDonald. Once he started, he could not stop.

Before long Big Alex owned a total of forty claims—a figure that astonished the citizens of Dawson. McDonald did not look

A group of women, claim-owners, and hired workmen gather around an elaborate set of sluiceboxes during spring clean-up.

like a shrewd buyer. A large, quiet man, he appeared uncomfortable with his awkward size. Whenever he was presented with a new mining offer, McDonald slowly rubbed his big hand across his chin and his thick, black mustache. He first answered "no" to each proposition, giving himself time to ponder matters alone. Despite his lack of social grace, McDonald soon became known as King of the Klondike, and his reputation spread throughout the world.

          ·····

Dawson was overflowing with people. In one year the population had soared from 1,500 to 30,000. Only a short time earlier Dawson was no more than a few tents and a moose pasture. Now, it was one of the largest cities in Canada. Every day more people joined the crowds that pushed up and down Front Street, the main avenue of town.

Most newcomers who plodded along Front Street were listless and dazed. It was difficult to imagine that these were the same men who had fought their way, wild-eyed and determined, across the mountain passes. Many had spent their life savings on the trip north and could not afford a steamship ticket home. Others were too ashamed of their failure to return to their families. So they continued to wander the muddy streets of the city, as if waiting for an answer to drop out of the sky.

The weather in Dawson did not help to soothe the restless cheechakos. While the winters were bitterly cold in the Klondike, the summers were unbearably hot. Because the northern regions of the globe tilt closer toward the sun in the summer, the Yukon Territory remains light almost twenty-four hours a day. Even at midnight during this season, it remains bright outside. The city of Dawson never seemed to sleep during the months of the midnight sun. The boundaries of town constantly expanded and the streets were always in the midst of change.

More and more businesses opened as practical people realized that they could become rich without ever lifting a shovel. By midsummer of 1898, Dawson had an undertaker, a palmreader, a steambath, two newspapers, and two banks. The

When the newcomers realized that gold claims were scarce in the Klondike, many simply roamed the streets of Dawson, wondering what to do next.

Bank of Commerce opened for business in a windowless warehouse that had previously been used for storing fish. Dozens of miners allowed their sacks of nuggets to be placed in the bank's vaults, which were two wooden chests at the back of a room.

The number of stores in Dawson was also increasing. It was becoming much easier to bring in goods to sell from the Outside. In the late spring of 1898, workers had finished building an aerial tramway over the Chilkoot Pass. Using a system of cables and pulleys run by steam engines, the tramway hoisted loads of supplies through the air in huge metal buckets. To make travel on the Chilkoot and White pass routes even smoother, steamboats now ran from the lakes at the foot of the mountains to Dawson. Stampeders who could afford the steamboat ticket avoided building their own crafts and facing the perilous waters.

As large shipments of goods arrived from the Outside, the waterfront began to look like a bustling bazaar. Rows of booths lined the shore, with every item imaginable for sale. One could

Stampeders gathered at the waterfront to sell their supplies. Some needed money to survive in Dawson. Others sold their entire outfits so they could return home.

buy anything from fresh grapes and ice-cream freezers to safety pins and peacock feathers.

Fine hotels began to rise up along Front Street. One of these was the Fairview, a grand, three-story building opened by a woman named Belinda Mulrooney. Belinda had come to the Klondike in 1897 at a time when few women had dared to venture into the northern wilderness. While other newcomers headed for Dawson, Belinda became one of the first settlers at Grand Forks, a small mining community at the fork of Bonanza and Eldorado creeks about fourteen miles from Dawson. Knowing there would be a need for lodging in the upcoming months, she supervised the construction of the Grand Forks Hotel. This building, which was made from logs, mud, and moss, was an instant success with the miners. However, Belinda was not completely satisfied. She wanted to build another hotel in Dawson—the most elegant hotel in the Klondike.

Belinda ordered all of the best furnishings for her new hotel—the Fairview—from the Outside. Then she went to supervise the men who had been hired to haul the wagonloads of

fragile supplies over the White Pass. To her dismay, she discovered the workers had abandoned her equipment on the trail after receiving a better offer to take a load of whiskey to Dawson. Belinda was furious. She hired another crew, and quickly set out to get her revenge. Belinda caught the culprits heading back up the trail with the whiskey loaded on a convoy of mules. She watched triumphantly as her men knocked out the foreman and threw the casks of whiskey down in the mud. Soon Belinda was on her way, her precious hotel supplies riding safely on the backs of the mules.

With the new shipment of furnishings, the Fairview was complete. No one could argue that any hotel was finer. The Fairview had thirty steam-heated guest rooms, brass beds, and Turkish baths. In the dining room the tables were spread with linen cloths, delicate china, and sterling silver. An orchestra played in the lobby under the gleam of cut-glass chandeliers.

By Klondike standards, Belinda had achieved perfection— except for one unmistakable flaw: the walls in the hotel were not made of wood or plaster. Only thin canvas with a covering of wallpaper separated the rooms. A guest could not even whisper

Belinda Mulrooney's Fairview was known as the finest hotel in the Klondike. It was the first inn in Dawson to offer guests brass beds and real sheets.

without being heard next door. Even with this shortcoming, the Fairview made Belinda rich. On grand opening night, the hotel bar brought in $6,000.

Saloons were the center of social life in Dawson. Whenever the lonely miners found any free time, they spent most of it in the lively bars along Front Street. These establishments, with their ornate entrances and plain interiors, offered customers whiskey, gambling, dancing, theater, and most of all, a chance to escape the hardships of life in the Klondike.

The theaters in Dawson presented a wide variety of entertainment on their tiny stages. The audiences never knew what sort of performers to expect. Some nights there were wrestling matches and acrobatic shows. Other nights there were serious dramas. At a saloon called the Palace Grand, Arizona Charlie occasionally demonstrated his target-shooting skills. The crowd cheered as he shot small glass balls from the hands of his lovely wife. But the miners' favorite acts were usually those that were the least complicated. They were especially fond of the Oatley sisters, who sang in clear, high voices. The audience fell completely silent when Lottie and Polly sang familiar ballads. Many

Many Klondikers lost their entire fortunes at the gambling tables within just a few hours of their find.

A dance-hall girl poses playfully for the camera.

men had to wipe the tears from their faces as they thought of their families far away.

While hard, wooden benches served as seats for the theater audience, the finer spots in the balcony were reserved for the wealthy mining kings. Throughout the show, the cheechakos on the ground floor would turn to catch a glimpse of the legendary Klondikers in the shadowy, curtained boxes. Like sightseers, they pointed out the richest claim-owners who sipped from forty-dollar bottles of champagne.

One theatergoer who always attracted stares was a comical little man called Swiftwater Bill Gates. Swiftwater's rise from poverty to prosperity had been quick and showy. He had worked as a dishwasher, until he suddenly struck it rich on Eldorado Creek. Before his share of gold was brought out of the ground, he began parading about town in a formal coat with tails, a top hat, and a diamond stickpin in his tie.

Swiftwater became famous for his frivolous spending and his efforts to impress the dance-hall girls. When he fell in love

with one young beauty named Gussie Lamore, it seemed that he would go to any lengths to please her. He promised to pay Gussie her weight in Eldorado gold if she would agree to marry him the next morning. Gussie took the money, but put off the marriage. She was only interested in this tiny man, with his scraggly black mustache and his starched white collar, for his money.

While Swiftwater and Gussie remained companions, they quarreled constantly. One argument in particular captured the attention of Dawson and was described by Klondike storytellers for years to come. According to an old-timer named Arthur Walden, Swiftwater was having breakfast in a restaurant one morning when Gussie entered on the arm of a gambler. Swiftwater was enraged. Before Gussie could order her favorite breakfast of fried eggs, he notified the chef and bought up every egg in the kitchen—at a cost of $600. The chef delivered the tempting platters of eggs, fried crisp and hot, to Swiftwater's table. Then, as Gussie watched in anger, Swiftwater pitched the delicacies, one by one, out the window to the pack of hungry dogs below.

Swiftwater Bill and his adventures were so amusing that they became the subjects of several theater productions in Dawson. Swiftwater often attended the plays, taking his place in a special box seat. The audience laughed uproariously at the antics on stage, but Swiftwater did not mind. He applauded enthusiastically as the actors took their bows, thrilled to be the center of so much attention.

When the theater performance was over, the miners' favorite part of the evening began. The wooden benches were pushed back against the wall and a four-piece orchestra appeared, transforming the playhouse into a dance hall. The miners paid a dollar to waltz with one of the women who worked in the saloon. Some men bought dozens of dance tickets in advance, not wanting to miss one promenade or polka.

The dancing in the saloons was organized by a caller, who stood on the stage and bellowed instructions in a loud, coaxing voice. "Come on, boys—let's have a nice, long waltz," the caller cried. "Fire away!" he yelled to the musicians. With their faces flushed and boots stomping, the miners began to swing their

partners around the floor. No sooner had the couples made two or three laps around the room, than the caller shouted for the dance to end and the patrons gathered at the bar.

The miners usually paid for drinks from small sacks of gold dust called pokes, which they hung inside their shirts. They tossed their leather pouches on the bar, and the saloon-keeper weighed out the price of a drink on a set of scales. So much gold changed hands that, at the end of the night, a fine sprinkling of gold dust covered the floor. A bartender could often pan a handsome profit from the dirt he swept up in the morning.

The miners not only bought whiskey and waltzes, but they tipped the most charming dance-hall girls with gold nuggets. The girls then sewed the biggest nuggets onto belts, which they proudly buckled on their waists like medals. As the hours wore on, the miners' pokes grew lighter. All night long the fiddlers played and the couples galloped around the dance floor. Even when the exhausted customers left at dawn, the saloons still did not close. They remained open around-the-clock every day—except Sunday.

Sunday was a day of rest in Dawson. No labor of any kind was permitted, by order of the North West Mounted Police. The

In the Klondike, customers paid for goods or services with gold. To make a purchase, miners poured gold dust from their pokes, and the correct amount was weighed out on scales.

The North West Mounted Police brought law and order to the Klondike.

mounties enforced the rule as strictly as they laid down laws against murder or robbery. From midnight on Saturday until two A.M. on Monday, the police patrolled the streets. They made sure that businesses were closed, saloons stayed empty, and Dawson's citizens remained as peaceful as housecats. There were no exceptions to the rules. One man was arrested for sawing wood on Sunday. Another was even fined for fishing.

The mounties, in their scarlet jackets, gold buttons, and tall polished boots, were respected by every man and woman in the Klondike. Most people had arrived in Dawson expecting a wild and lawless town. However, very few crimes took place. Pistols or handguns were forbidden in Dawson, and in 1898 not a single murder was committed. Thefts were also rare. As one goldseeker wrote, "For days and days I could leave milk tins

Before an efficient postal system was established in the Klondike, the overworked North West Mounted Police were also in charge of handling the mail. Klondikers sometimes waited for hours to shuffle through hundreds of letters searching for their mail.

By 1898, many women worked alongside their husbands and mining partners on the gold claims.

filled with gold dust, and my watch, rifle, and claim papers alone in my cabin unlocked and I never lost anything."

The Mounted Police were also responsible for controlling less serious crimes. It was not permissible to cheat at cards, use bad language, sell liquor to dance-hall girls, or behave in a disorderly way in public. Those who committed these offenses were punished with fines, or even worse, back-breaking labor on the government woodpile. As many as fifty prisoners were kept busy at all times splitting firewood to heat the Mounted Police barracks. However, the most severe sentence of all was a "blue ticket." Blue-ticket criminals were forced to leave Dawson and never return. For men who had spent months reaching the Klondike and were finally lucky enough to stake a claim, this was the ultimate punishment.

Although Dawson had never been a violent place, the growing presence of law and order in the Klondike could not be missed. The Mounted Police brought organization and stability to the hectic days of the gold rush. As the Klondike grew calmer, miners sent for their wives and children. Dawson was no longer just a mining town. For many, it was becoming a home. ❧

By the end of the gold rush, wealthy Klondikers were bringing more and more luxuries north. This family's parlor includes a piano, wallpaper, and carpets. The father even holds a Seattle newspaper on his lap—another reminder that Dawson was no longer cut off from the Outside.

V

After the Rush

P erhaps the early-day miners in Dawson knew that times had truly changed when the first tourists arrived in town. In the summer of 1898, two wealthy ladies stepped off a steamboat with plans to take in the sights of Dawson for a month or two. One was Mrs. Mary Hitchcock, the wife of an admiral in the United States Navy. The other was Miss Edith Van Buren, the daughter of former U.S. President Martin Van Buren.

Mrs. Hitchcock and Miss Van Buren intended to leave the North by September, when a chill usually crept into the air. However, they brought enough baggage to satisfy their whims for a year. Their luggage included two dogs, two canaries, two dozen pigeons, a talking parrot, a mandolin, a record player, and a portable bowling alley. The women had no problem finding a place to put these extravagant possessions. They had also brought along an enormous tent, which was the size of twenty log cabins and weighed more than 400 pounds.

The two tourists were the talk of Dawson, with their grand belongings and "high society" ways. When the ladies invited Big Alex McDonald to an elegant dinner party in their giant tent, *The Klondike Nugget* reported the evening a spectacular success. The guests had dined on a delicious four-course meal served by a miner dressed in a white waiter's jacket. The menu consisted of mock-turtle soup, lobster, leg of mutton, potato balls, scal-

loped tomatoes, asparagus salad, peach ice cream, and black coffee.

The peaceful days that Mrs. Hitchcock and Miss Van Buren enjoyed in Dawson did not last for long. At six o'clock on the morning of October 15, a police bugle sounded. A dance-hall girl had left a candle burning in her room at the Green Tree Saloon. The muslin curtains caught fire and within minutes several buildings on Front Street were wrapped in flames. As the fire ripped through the post office and the hotel next door, men ran for the city's new fire engines. But the equipment, which had not yet been paid for, still sat packed in crates.

Soon three long lines of men were passing buckets of water from the Yukon River to the burning streets. By the time a former fire chief of Seattle assembled the pumps and hoses, the bucket brigade had already brought the fire under control. The gathering crowd cheered as the last flames flickered out. Then

During the fire of April 1899, volunteers tried to stop the blaze by draping wet blankets over buildings in the path of the flames. Despite these attempts, Dawson was almost entirely destroyed.

A group of townspeople watch helplessly as flames sweep through the McDonald Hotel.

the smoke slowly cleared, revealing the ashes and charred remains of forty buildings that had been destroyed.

Frightened by the threat of another disaster, the leaders of Dawson began to institute public safety programs the very next day. A fire department was formed and 100 men rushed to join. With contributions from the dance-hall girls, the city raised enough money to pay for the fire engines. The entire town felt a sense of relief, watching the new firefighters drill and train. But on the night of April 26, 1899, it happened again.

Despite months of preparation, Dawson was not ready for the worst accident in its history. When the flames leaped out of the window in the Bodega Saloon on First Avenue, the firemen

On special holidays, firemen from the Dawson Fire Department demonstrated their skills. Here, a group of firefighters pull a heavy roll of hoses down the street.

were away from their posts. Days before, the crew had asked for a raise. The town council refused, and the department went on strike. Usually, workers were appointed to keep the boilers in the fire engines burning. Others were stationed at the Yukon River to make sure the water holes did not clog with ice. During the strike, the boilers went cold and the river froze solid, cutting off the water supply.

At the waterfront, volunteers set bonfires on the ice, desperately trying to melt through the surface. Meanwhile, the flames rose higher as the fire spread, and an orange-red glow filled the night sky. Dance-hall girls ran screaming from the saloons, with their flouncy skirts gathered under their arms. Hundreds of people frantically dashed through the rooms of endangered buildings, grabbing up anything valuable in sight. Although the fire singed their eyelashes and burned their cheeks,

most did not feel the intense heat. The temperature outside was 45 degrees below zero.

Many firemen had raced back to their jobs and stood waiting impatiently for their hoses to fill with water. The wait was agony for the property owners who watched the fire creep closer to their buildings. Flames leaped from street to street, but still no water came. Then, suddenly, the onlookers heard a horrible, ripping sound—the sound of hoses bursting. The boilers had not been hot enough to heat the cold river water being pumped to the fire. The water had frozen before reaching the nozzles, and the thick chunks of ice tore open the hoses.

The townspeople were convinced that Dawson was lost. Yet there was one possible solution left to try: dynamite. Perhaps if the buildings in front of the fire were blown up with explosives, the flames would have nothing left to feed upon and simply die out. The North West Mounted Police ran to get fifty pounds of blasting powder, which they placed at carefully chosen points in the path of the blaze. The dynamite was lit, and Dawson shook with the powerful blast. Big Alex McDonald watched his brand new office building explode into bits.

The townspeople realized their efforts were useless when the fire continued in spite of the explosion. Flames blackened the beautiful furnishings of Belinda Mulrooney's Fairview Hotel. In the Bank of British North America, the safes shot open with the intense heat. Gold bricks and nuggets burst from the vaults and melted in the burning coals on the ground. Hours later the fire finally died, leaving 117 buildings in ashes and one million dollars' worth of damage behind.

Dawson began to rebuild even before the embers had stopped smoldering. Within weeks newly completed stores and saloons were serving customers as if the disaster had never occurred. While business continued as usual after the fire, the town changed drastically in other ways. Dawson lost the rough and reckless look of its early gold rush days. Sturdy, wooden sidewalks were laid down where muddy paths had once been. Two-story houses, with parlors and curtains in the windows, replaced tents and log cabins. Schools and steepled churches appeared. Many of the new buildings even had electricity and telephones.

By 1899, Dawson was no longer a tent town. Klondikers began to build large two-story homes with glass windows and front porches.

Another dramatic change was taking place on the White Pass. In the summer of 1899, workers finished laying the last piece of track on the new railroad from Skagway to Lake Bennett. The White Pass & Yukon Railway would eventually stretch all the way to Whitehorse, a small settlement upriver from Dawson. Now passengers could ride in comfort over the steep mountain, where thousands of horses once stumbled and fell to their deaths.

Although it was easier to get to the Klondike, the gold rush had passed its peak. The waterfront had calmed and the streets were no longer filled with newcomers. People began to turn their attention to building a solid community. They organized social

clubs, opened a library, and held charity balls for the new hospital. But just when Dawson was becoming more stable, news arrived that turned the city upside-down.

Throughout the spring of 1899, the townspeople had heard rumors about a rich gold discovery made somewhere in Alaska. In June a sailor who had just returned from the new diggings brought word that the rumors were true. Prospectors had discovered a fortune on the beaches of Nome, Alaska, an area located 1,800 miles west of Dawson near the mouth of the Yukon River. According to witnesses, the gold from Nome was the finest and purest found anywhere in the North.

The old-timers were the first to set out for the diggings on the coast of the Bering Sea. Many had become impatient as they watched Dawson transform into "the San Francisco of the North." They longed for the solitude and adventure of unex-

A group of schoolchildren gather with their teacher in Dawson. During spring clean-up season, schools in the Klondike often closed so that children could help on the claims.

plored lands. Quietly, the restless prospectors slipped away to Alaska.

Like a familiar tune, the stampede was beginning once again. The newspapers were splashed with bold headlines announcing each bit of news from Nome. Saloons and street corners buzzed with excitement. Log cabins and businesses were going up for sale. Almost every day, a new steamship packed with passengers headed up the Yukon River for Alaska. During one week in August, 8,000 people left Dawson to find more promising rewards.

The Klondike gold rush ended—just three years after the incredible adventure had begun.

<hr/>

Although nearly 40,000 people reached Dawson during the Klondike gold rush, only several hundred were lucky enough to find large amounts of gold. And of these miners only a handful remained wealthy in the years following the great stampede. Countless men and women had set out for the Klondike with barely enough money in their pockets to buy a full meal or a new suit of clothes. Those who suddenly became rich claim-owners often could not resist spending their money in frivolous ways. They squandered their wealth on needless luxuries, glamorous trips, and unwise business deals. Some men lost fortunes at the gambling tables within hours after digging the gold from the ground.

Big Alex McDonald, the "King of the Klondike," became one of the many miners who watched their riches disappear. While most men left for Nome, McDonald remained in Dawson and continued to buy more claims. Gradually, his obsession for land began to outweigh his desire for gold. In fact, gold became so meaningless to Big Alex that he kept a heaping bowl of nuggets in his house and casually offered visitors their pick of the pile. He devoted all of his money and attention to purchasing more property, giving little thought to the value of the claims. Soon it became clear that McDonald's vast stretches of land were worthless and his fortune had melted away.

McDonald lived his last years alone in a humble cabin on Clearwater Creek. One day a miner passed by and found McDonald's body lying on the ground. Big Alex had died of a heart attack while chopping wood.

Although Belinda Mulrooney lived much longer than Big Alex McDonald, she shared his financial fate. At the height of the gold rush, Belinda was admired throughout the Klondike for

During her wealthy days, the stylish Belinda Mulrooney poses with her husband, Charles Eugene Carbonneau.

her strong business sense and her clever ways. The most eligible bachelors in Dawson constantly tried to win her affections. But Belinda refused all advances—until Charles Eugene Carbonneau came to town.

Carbonneau arrived stylishly, accompanied by a personal servant and sporting a walking cane and a curled, black mustache. He passed out business cards, introducing himself as both a royal count and a salesman of fine French champagne. Immediately, Carbonneau began to call upon Belinda and send her a bouquet of red roses every day. Belinda did not care when a miner recognized the so-called Count Carbonneau as a barber from the Canadian city of Montreal. In October of 1900, the couple married and settled near Dawson.

Despite a romantic courtship, the Carbonneau marriage did not last long. Six years later Belinda and her husband were divorced. Once again independent, Belinda built a huge stone mansion, which she called the Castle, in Washington State. But gradually, the fortune Belinda had earned in the Klondike began to disappear. She sold the Castle and later moved to a nursing home near Seattle. Belinda died at the age of ninety-five, penniless—but rich with memories of her heyday in Dawson.

While many well-known miners were never heard of after 1899, the newspapers often followed the whereabouts of the Klondike's original discoverers. After their strike on Bonanza Creek, George Washington Carmack, Skookum Jim, and Tagish Charley remained together for a short time. They took a lavish trip to Seattle to spend their gold, reserving a suite of rooms in one of the finest hotels. Carmack's Indian wife, Kate, had never ventured out of the Yukon and was completely confused by city life. To her, the hotel's winding staircases and dark hallways were like a bewildering maze. Kate finally brought out her hunting knife and marked a trail in the mahogany wood so she could find her way back to her room. Along with Jim and Charley, Kate continued to shock the citizens of Seattle. The three entertained themselves by throwing nuggets from the hotel window and watching the people below scramble between the horses' hooves and wagon wheels to get the gold.

Meanwhile, Carmack was happily enjoying the luxuries of

In 1899, mining machinery gradually began to replace picks and shovels. Although the machines were more efficient, they ripped through the Klondike soil and left the countryside bare and scarred.

the Outside. He began to plan a yacht trip around the world—a journey that would carry him far away from his Indian friends. In 1900 Carmack divorced Kate and soon after married a fashionable woman named Marguerite Laimee. Unlike most Klondike miners, Carmack lived the rest of his days in financial comfort.

When Carmack departed on his cruise, the Indians also went separate ways. Although Skookum Jim made huge sums of money each year from his Bonanza claim, he did not retire from mining. He spent the rest of his life prospecting, hoping to make a big discovery that he could call his own. Tagish Charley sold his claim in 1901 and lived wildly on the profits. One holiday season, he fell from a bridge on the White Pass Railroad, and drowned.

During the uproar of the gold rush, Robert Henderson was not totally forgotten. The Canadian government eventually recognized him as a co-discoverer of the Klondike and paid him a sum of $200 a month for life to reward his contribution to the country. Yet this recognition was not enough for Henderson. He continued to search for gold throughout Canada, until he died at the age of seventy-six. Henderson never found a strike to equal the wealth of Bonanza Creek.

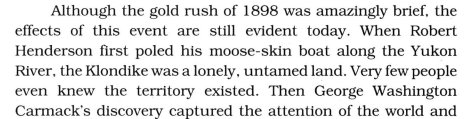

Although the gold rush of 1898 was amazingly brief, the effects of this event are still evident today. When Robert Henderson first poled his moose-skin boat along the Yukon River, the Klondike was a lonely, untamed land. Very few people even knew the territory existed. Then George Washington Carmack's discovery captured the attention of the world and *Klondike* became an everyday word.

As stampeders confidently set out on untraveled routes to the Klondike, a transformation took place in the North. On their way to Dawson, many stampeders discovered fertile ground for farming. Others stumbled upon creeks showing traces of gold. Men and women cut their journeys short and stayed to develop the land. As if a hidden door had been flung open, the mystery

Thousands of men and women returned to their normal lives after the Klondike gold rush, but their outlook on the world had changed profoundly. The stampede taught those who reached Dawson that they could survive hardships and make a home in a desolate land— achievements that had seemed impossible only a few months before.

surrounding Alaska and northwest Canada disappeared. Suddenly, the North was a frontier for opportunity.

Few mining fortunes were made in the Klondike. In the early days comforts were rare and hardships were common. Yet, most of those who took part in this strange mass movement northward continued to share one special thought until they died: they would not have missed the Klondike adventure for anything in the world. 🕭

Glossary

blue ticket   a punishment given by the North West Mounted Police, ordering serious criminals to leave town permanently

cheechako   a Chinook Indian word meaning "newcomer." The term soon became widely used in the Klondike to describe newly arrived stampeders with little mining experience.

claim   a portion of land used for mining. By Canadian law, a claim could only be 500 feet long and 100 feet wide. To "stake" or declare himself owner of a claim during the gold rush, a miner had to pay an entry fee of fifteen dollars and another fee for each additional year he kept the claim. Miners also were required to pay government taxes on all gold they found.

grubstake   supplies or money given to a prospector to finance his search for gold in exchange for a share of the profits

outfit   the food and equipment needed for a mining trip

poke   a small leather pouch or bag used by miners and other Klondikers to hold gold dust

riffles   a set of narrow poles which fitted into the bottom of sluice-boxes and trapped the gold dust as it washed by

roadhouse   a hotel or restaurant located along the trail or outside of town. Besides meals and a place to sleep, many roadhouses also offered dancing and gambling.

84

sawpit   a raised platform used for sawing logs into planks. To produce boards for boats in the Klondike, one man stood on the platform, while another took his place underneath. Each worker held the handle of a long, hook-tooth saw and guided the tool up and down through the logs.

sluicebox   a narrow wooden box, usually measuring about twelve feet long, with open ends. Miners shoveled gold-bearing dirt into the upper end, then channeled stream water through the open passage. As the dirt and gravel washed away, the fine gold dust was left behind in the riffles on the bottom of the boxes.

spring clean-up   the period in the mining season when piles of dirt were washed through sluiceboxes to separate the gold. Each spring, the miners waited for the snow and icy creeks to thaw, which would allow them to wash out the gold-bearing dirt they had collected during the fall and winter.

tramway   a carrier that travels on an overhead cable. In the spring of 1898, workers finished constructing the longest tramway in the Klondike, which hauled stampeders' supplies over the Chilkoot Pass in large buckets.

whipsawing   the process of cutting logs into narrow boards with a long, two-man saw (see *sawpit*)

Yukon Order of the Pioneers   an organization of miners and prominent businessmen. This club was established at the settlement of Forty Mile in the Yukon Territory in 1894.

Index

Page numbers in *italics* refer to illustrations

Picture Credits

—————⟫◦◦◦◦◦◦◯◦◦◦◦◦◦⟪—————

The photographs in this book are from the following sources and are used with their permission:

Courtesy of Alaska Northwest Publishing Company, Seattle, Washington • page 27.

The Museum of History and Industry, Seattle, Washington • pages 20, 22-23.

Provincial Archives of British Columbia • pages 36-37: photo no. HP67007.

The Ronald C. Kinsey Collection • pages 4, 13, 19, 52, 57, 66-67, 69, 70, 76, 81: all photos by Kinsey & Kinsey.

The Seattle Times • page 79.

Alaska and Polar Regions Department, University of Alaska, Fairbanks, Alaska • page 63: photographer unknown, University of Washington negative no. 9228; page 73: photo by Goetzman, University of Washington negative no. 3017; page 74: photo by Goetzman, University of Washington negative no. 3033.

Special Collections Division, University of Washington Libraries, Seattle, Washington • page ii: photo by Hegg, negative no. 3209; pages 6-7: photo by Hegg, negative no. 2292; page 8: photo by A. Curtis, negative no. 62086; page 14: photographer unknown, negative no. 8277; page 16: photographer unknown, negative no. 7940; page 28: photographer unknown, negative no. 7807; page 30: photo by Cantwell, negative no. 33; page 32: photo by Hegg, negative no. 130; page 34: photo by Wilse, negative no. 20; page 38: photo by Curtis, negative no. 46009; page 39: photo by Curtis, negative no. 1339; page 40: photo by Goetzman, negative no. 117; page 41: photo by Curtis, negative no. 46112; page 42: photo by La Roche, negative no. 2014; page 43: photo by Cantwell, negative no. 37; page 45: photo by Hirshfeld, negative no. 13; page 48: photo by Cantwell, negative no. 39; page 49: photo by Hegg, negative no. 229; page 50: photo by Goetzman, negative no. 134; page 51: photo by Child, negative no. 17; page 54: photo by Curtis, negative no. 46131; page 56: photo by Curtis, negative no. 46078; page 60: photo by Curtis, negative no 46068; page 61: photo by Ellingsen, negative no. 41; page 62: photo by Goetzman, negative no. 3019; page 65: photo by Larss & Duclos, negative no. 1; page 68: photo by Hegg, negative no. 346; page 72: photo by Hegg, negative no. 2214; page 77: photo by Hegg, negative no. 458.

Vancouver Public Library • page 59.

Yukon Archives, Whitehorse, Yukon Territory • page vi: from the Henderson Family Collection; page 10 (left): Macbride Museum Collection; page 10 (right): Skookum Jim Oral History Project Collection; page 46: Gillis Collection.